not gonna die in the dark

episode

1

story and art
by

adam archer

not gonna die in the dark: episode 1

Text and illustrations © 2018 by Adam Archer

First Printing February 2018

Edited by E.K. Eoff

The author is responsible for any liberties

taken with grammar and punctuation :)

Find all of the authors books on Amazon and Barnes and Noble.

Visit the author on Twitter, Instagram, and Facebook.

1

A breeze stirred the grass at Maggie's feet and flipped up the corner of her Bristol board. The girl had been holding the drawing pad upside down—to get a more natural curve for the outline of a head—and forgot to hold the unbound side of the pages with her other hand. The edge of the thick paper clacked against her pencil, startling the girl and ruining her line. With her heart beating faster, Maggie turned the tool over, erased the wind's crooked contribution, and started again.

That should not *have freaked me out that much,* she thought. *Hopefully I was just out to lunch and in the zone.*

She looked down at her bare shins and the long blades of grass that tapped against them. The girl had sprayed her lower half generously with repellent to keep the ticks (and hopefully their crippling diseases) at bay. The sour smell of the pungent chemicals was still strong as it drifted up off the granite stones beneath her.

Heart's pumping like I'm running from a tiger. You're in a field, sitting on your butt, drawing. Settle down girl. Let's toughen up a bit hunh?

Abandoning the misshapen head, Maggie drew two large circles in the space beneath it. This turned the stylized chipmunk she had been drawing for a freelance job into a ridiculously busty bucktoothed rodent. She chuckled.

They'll either laugh or never hire me again. Knowing the editors, probably the latter.

She drew cross-eyes nipples for the hell of it, smiled, and then totally erased the chest balloons. She decided to keep the first round of pencil submissions family-friendly. You don't joke around with people without a funny bone, not if you liked being employed, and Maggie needed the money.

The girl had been drawing for Looksee Toys for just over a year—two weeks actually before she received her driver's license. Like every job she landed as an artist, whether toy designs, spot illustrations, or commissioned pieces from her followers online, it meant a lot to her. Maggie knew that soon her life would be changing—or hoped it would be—so it had been an intentional goal to save aggressively for some time. Her plan was to get by at school, illustrate to bring in money, and then get out of the situation she was in. It required some planning, some discipline, and quite a bit of hope, but the girl was focused, and often surprised herself with the progress.

Sighing, Maggie rubbed the back of her neck.

Okay I'm really *not feeling this chipmunk guy. But that's freelance right? Get it done, even when your mind's all over the place.*

She scooted up to the next-highest boulder on the granite hill and looked around. The sun was getting low, and everything in sight was lit with a surreal amber glow.

Maggie exhaled slowly and her forearms tingled. She had always breathed shallowly when drawing, holding her breath for precision and subconsciously rationing air to her lungs. The sporadic deep breaths she *did* manage usually brought tingles, reminding her of what she had been doing.

Enjoy these moments, she thought. *No mosquitoes. The trippy lighting. Little good things.*

Life had shown Maggie that the big victories were tough

to come by, and too often were nowhere to be found. For that reason, she made a conscious effort to hold on to the small things, the nice things, to remember them whenever she could in the hope that any glance at the past might provide at least a little light. This, in turn, might inspire confidence in things to come. That was the plan, at least, and any courage she could muster would be precious indeed if she were ever able to leave home.

"All right," she said aloud, "take a breath girl. You're drawing like you have no friggin' idea." She turned the page to start fresh, but frowned when the Bristol flipped over and made a strange sound. After a pause, Maggie heard it again. But it wasn't the paper. Turning, the girl saw that she wasn't alone.

"I'm sorry, but who the *hell* are you talking to?" Stephanie Fricklin asked. The girl was standing off to the side at the base of the granite hill.

Maggie's heart skipped a beat. She had always hated surprises. "I'm reciting my lines for a play," she said, as calmly as she could manage.

Stephanie looked confused. "You're not *in* drama class."

Maggie shrugged. "I'm not in a play. I was just talking to myself."

Stephanie nodded and looked at the surrounding trees. "That's about right." She, too, was a junior, though in a different clique. Maggie had always unintentionally walked the line between nerdy and popular, usually feeling more at home with the squares. Stephanie wasn't in that group.

The girl turned back to Maggie and smiled. "I can see the wheels turning under that white hair. Wondering what I'm doing here?"

"Definitely," Maggie said. "My guess is you're lost."

"Nope. I came here on purpose. In fact I just chatted with your dad since I was looking for you, and he seemed a little pissed off that I brought you up."

Softly, Maggie said, "Par for the course," and turned back to her page.

"You're still talking to yourself."

Maggie shrugged again.

"Look, I don't want to come out and rant on about how

awkward you make every encounter, even though I kind of am right now." Stephanie paused and rubbed her chin. It was the first hint of her appearing unsure, at least the first one that Maggie had noticed so far. "Aiden wants to walk around tonight...but he's bringing Tony."

A little lightbulb went off in Maggie's head. The pretty girl traipsing across a field for the less popular semi-closet-case was starting to make sense. Maggie smiled at the absurdity of it. "Your boyfriend's buddy needs someone to walk around with, and you pick *me*?" She laughed. "*No* one picks me. Is every other girl in town sick or something? They have to be dead right?"

"Long story," said Stephanie. "And I'm not gonna bullshit you or kiss your ass. You want to come out or not?"

Maggie raised an eyebrow. "I get it. I'm the skinny, gawky nerd supposed to tag along so there's no outshining done. You just need a warm body to play sidekick."

"Maggie, you're not *ugly*. If you were, Tony wouldn't bother coming out."

"Ouch. Lie to me Stephanie. I thought I was being humble. You know, it's easier making fun of myself than to hear it...put like that."

"Sorry. No bullshit."

Maggie knew what walking around at night meant, or *thought* she did. She had cruised the neighborhoods a few times her sophomore year at overnight parties, and almost everything that went on then was awkward, experimental, or nothing to be proud of. She closed the sketch pad on her unfinished drawing and dropped the pencil in her bag. When she spoke again, her answer surprised them both, and maybe, in part, that was why she said, "Yes."

2

He moved noiselessly through the brush, or nearly so. The gentle tug of branches across his coat, and the moist leaves compressing beneath his feet, were the only things disturbed. More importantly, the insignificant sounds from these movements went unnoticed by the only living creature around.

She was forty, or just shy of it; he could see this clearly enough in the day's waning light. The shadow at her feet and that of the mailbox beside her were fading, blending into others as night drew near.

But she wasn't right. She was in some ways, in ways that would merit a second glance, but after a closer look—no. The dark hair, and her gait; the way she moved was forgettable. Not the same. He lowered his head and didn't see the mailbox open, but heard it. She took something out, though what it was didn't matter. He stayed beneath a diseased oak where the shadows would soon deepen. He would remain there, unmoving, at least for a while.

3

The streetlights came on with a hum as Maggie stepped from the grassy field. After looking for cars, she jogged across the street and then hopped up to the curb on the other side.

Why did I say yes though? She shook her head. *I'm not even* into *that stuff. Hanging out? Who am I kidding?* She tucked a bouncing lock of hair behind her ear. *Guilt. That's why. Life's blowing by and I feel like I haven't done anything yet. I'm partying out of* guilt. She laughed softly. *Gotta rethink my priorities. Be true to myself and be okay with it. But I'll start tomorrow right?*

"Your posture's worse than mine."

The girl looked up. She couldn't see a face, but Maggie knew the voice. "Hey Mrs. Carson." She turned to the dark screened-in porch a few yards away.

"It's all the computer tablets you guys play. You keep 'em on your lap and bring your heads down to *them*." The floorboards on the porch creaked as the woman drew near. "You should hold them above your heads. Then you'd all have the posture of ballerinas. 'Course that'd look strange, too."

Maggie shifted her messenger bag. "It's not from games, it's probably from reading. And I'm shy so I tend to turtle it up a bit anyway."

The door squeaked open as Mrs. Carson stepped out. The old woman leaned against the door frame and crossed her arms. "'Turtle it up.' Cute. I did that when I was young, but that was because I had a big bust and it would catch all the eyes. Don't know why the hell I was shy about that. Probably thought it'd attract the wrong men." The woman thumbed back in the direction of the house. "Well I guess it did. So much for that."

Maggie smiled politely. "Mr. Carson's a good man. I'm sure it's your personality that won him over."

Mrs. Carson chuckled. "Thank you honey. Nice of you to say but…you know, I don't think *Stanley's* even said that to me before. My personality hunh? Now I feel bad for *him*." She gave Maggie a wink. "You get home though before the mosquitoes carry you away. You don't have much to give."

With a wave, Maggie was off and down the street. After wiggling her fingers, she pulled her hands into her sleeves to keep them from the cool night air. She exhaled slowly and looked down. It was chilly, but not enough to see the cloudy vapors of her breath. She would try it again though, because it always seemed colder by her home.

A little more than half a block down, on the other side of the street, Maggie noticed someone on the curb rocking back and forth. At first, she thought it was a man, but after a second glance, the rough face of a woman could be seen through knotted oily hair. Beside that woman *was* a man, Maggie might very well have thought dead had it not been for his shaking left foot. The girl averted her gaze, hoping to avoid any interaction, but didn't turn before seeing that the man's pants were shredded and his genitals were exposed.

Oh shit, she thought, turning away. *Just flyin' on out there. Beautiful. I feel bad for these people but* dang.

Her hand slid into the small pouch at the front of her bag and clutched the one-ounce pepper spray canister inside. Two years before, there had been a double rape less than a hundred yards from Maggie's front door. The attackers had held the girls at knifepoint and ravaged them in the bushes just off the main street. Since then, Maggie was never without her little can of liquid fire.

Still walking, the girl pretended to glance up at a house on the left. With her peripheral vision, she saw that neither of the two had stood up from the sidewalk in an attempt to follow.

Maggie crossed the next street and jogged up the walkway to the front steps of 13 Nicoli Lane. Imagining footfalls behind her, she pulled open the storm door and jammed her house key into the large doorknob behind it. After a quick turn of the wrist, she shoved hard and half-fell inside. On springs almost ruined by time, the storm door swung closed abruptly, hitting the girl's back and pushing her the rest of the way in.

Maggie took a deep breath and leaned back against the thick wooden door. The click of the bolt sliding home into the frame was comforting, but a refuge this was not. Neither school nor home was a sanctuary—and hadn't been anything close to that since her mom had gone. Even thirteen years before, when all three Muntins had lived under one roof, things weren't exactly blissful. There had been some warmth in the house, at least when Maggie was very young, but the memories of a four-year-old were few. They were never an affectionate family—their Irish side got the blame for that—so hugs and other contact were rare. But a lack of fighting and raised voices (for the most part) at least allowed for some tranquil years. Though all this ended abruptly when the family split. In the absence of her mother, Maggie felt the steady weight of life's responsibilities slowly build. Yet even as this pressure increased, the girl was never the weakest link in what remained of her family. She suffered from self-doubt as much as anyone else, but at her core the girl was strong, and she never gave up. In part, this was due to who she was as a person; it was also because she didn't feel she had a choice. Her father, on the other hand, *had* given up. Maggie wanted nothing more than to be happy and have a good life. She saw hard work, and the constant struggle to build confidence, as a means to reach these goals. Her father, however, turned inward when his life changed. The man neglected both the things in his life and the people in it. He interacted less and less with the world as time passed, and hadn't pursued a job in nearly two years. His relationship with his daughter was nearly nonexistent, almost an intentional avoidance that was tough for Maggie to ignore. Because of this, the home was as cold as the crisp air outside; a place to be tolerated—at least until she could find the road to a good life.

Her father, Stewart Muntin, heard the girl enter (she saw his head move on the couch), but didn't turn around.

"Hey," Maggie said, but didn't get a response.

Oookay. Talk later. Must be some good TV. Daughter growing up behind you? Nope, he's good.

Each morning and afternoon she offered greetings, and rarely were they returned. This neglect stung; it wore her down a little inside. The girl had always at least tried to do what was right, for its own sake, not because of what the good actions might bring but because of how they made her feel, a little closer to the person she wanted to be. But this death-of-a-thousand-cuts home life had scarred and calloused her in too many ways. Maggie didn't like to think of it like that, but it had. The rebukes and slights were affecting her too much. They were adding up, and she was afraid they were lessening her ability—and in rare moments her desire—to take care of herself, and that wasn't acceptable.

4

Maggie walked past her father (and the TV he refused to let die) and headed for the stairs. In the last two years alone, the man had managed to burn through three projection bulbs in the older-model television. Where the money had come from to replace those bulbs, the girl didn't know, but her father did have his priorities.

A few pieces of mail dangled off the bottom step and Maggie scooped them up as she stepped past. Among them were a renewal notice for *Young Women Scouts Monthly* (a subscription she had received as a gift from a teacher when she was ten, now paid for herself, and wasn't ready to let go), an advertising mailer for butter-based makeup, and some other odds and ends.

The girl took the stairs two at a time and laid her bag on the floor just inside the doorway. She stooped to pull out her sketchbook and tossed both it and the mail on her bed. Scratching beneath her thick white locks, she sighed. Under that sketch cover was an unfinished drawing her client needed by the morning, while down the street was a group of not-quite-friends that might offer a way of avoiding the doldrums, at least for a time. It was ironic that Maggie's longtime passion for drawing—a sanity-saving pursuit—had become such a constant part of her life that she sometimes sought detours from it.

That's adulthood baby. But who am I kidding? Being an adult would mean staying home and doing the work. Sitting tight and getting it done.

Maggie rolled on some extra deodorant and picked up a cut-off jacket from the floor.

We'll call that perfume. She looked down at her sketch pad. *Maybe sometimes you have to do the wrong thing, so you can appreciate it when you do the right one.* She smiled. *Total crap, but I'll buy it tonight.*

With the jacket over her shoulder, the girl picked up her messenger bag, hurried down the stairs, and was out the door without a word to or from her father.

5

"Why the hell are we waiting?" Tony Bardou mumbled around a mouthful of chips. "We been out here—look." He held up an almost empty cup and sucked down the last of his Slushy. "I've finished *one* of these, and I'm ready to go in and get another. That's how long we've been waiting for her."

Aiden Binkers looked from the convenience store's gas pumps to his friend on the curb. He motioned to the store behind him. "Mr. Mullet inside isn't gonna *let* you back in. How many pumps of that syrup crap you put in there? Forty-two? You're gonna *die* dude. You're giving yourself diabetes right now. Good job."

"Whatever. I'm fine," Tony said, noisily slurping an empty cup. "Ooh—ice-headache. But I'm not gonna sit here with nothing to do. Another minute and I'm going in."

"Go for it," said Aiden. "But we might not be here when you come out."

"What about Maggie?"

"I got Steph."

Stephanie Fricklin slapped Aiden on the shoulder. "Like I'm a friggin' suitcase. 'He *has* me.' Nice."

Aiden winked and the girl rolled her eyes.

"Look," Tony said, "I'm no Don Juan, but why'd I get stuck with the elf chick?"

Aiden laughed. "Elf. Love it. 'Cause she's all twiny and ethereal right?"

Stephanie turned to Aiden. "Wait, what did you just say? Do you even know what that means?"

"Ethereal? Yeah. It's like ghostly or elfish or somethin'."

Stephanie raised an eyebrow. "Wow. I'm actually kinda impressed. That's a big word for someone who doesn't read."

Aiden pointed at her with both hands. "I watch movies hotcakes. There's some good stuff there."

"Don't call me that."

Tony chuckled. He then stood, deciding it was a good time for his second Slushy. The boy's hand was on the crossbar of the door when he glanced over his shoulder and saw a tall, thin silhouette approaching a streetlight. Maggie's hair nearly glowed when she reached that shining pool of light, while most of her face remained in shadow. "Here she is."

After muttered greetings, the group left the gas station

and walked off into the night.

Elmore Drive was less than ten minutes away, and first on Aiden's list of places to lurk after dark. The houses were set farther back from the road than most neighborhoods, so anyone on the street wasn't as easily noticed, especially at night.

Putting a hand in his coat pocket, Aiden said, "Anyone pissed you guys off recently?"

Stephanie looked up. "Is that a trick question?"

Aiden fake-laughed. He then took out his hand and held up two eggs.

Maggie frowned when she saw them.

Tony shook his head. "How the *hell* are you carrying around eggs in your pocket?"

Aiden reached into his jacket again. "Toilet paper tube." He pulled out the cardboard cylinder and flicked it at Tony's face.

It bonked off the boy's forehead and he cussed.

"Bet you can't hit a street sign from here," Maggie said.

"Those are pretty damn loud too."

Frowning, Aiden looked over at her. The boy was starting to breathe hard since Elmore Drive ran uphill. "You're a good girl aren't you? You just don't want me to hit somebody's house."

Looking to her right, Maggie saw a warm light seeping around the drawn curtains of a window. In her mind, the girl pictured a family on the other side sitting at the dinner table.

"I guess I don't *need* to," Maggie said. "I think I'd have to be pissed off at someone to do something like that. I'd need some reas—"

BAM! BAM!

The boys burst out laughing and sprinted uphill. It took Stephanie and Maggie only a moment to figure out what had happened.

The exterior lights of the house to their left came on as the front door began to open.

"Ah damn it," Stephanie said. "Come on!"

Maggie followed the other three up the hill and soon passed Tony, who was already walking and wheezing.

"Who the hell," Tony spat out, "runs away...*uphill?*"

Laughing, Aiden said, "*We* do! But did you see what I hit?"

"No."

"You didn't even *look?*"

Tony didn't answer; he just focused on breathing and not passing out.

"I was going to say you guys're twelve-year-olds," Stephanie said, "but they're all at home right now acting like adults."

"The garage door *and* the car," said Aiden. "And that shit's not good for paint."

Honestly wishing she were home, Maggie asked, "Whose house was it?"

"Uh some underclassman, no idea what his name is."

"I think it's Ass McAsslington," Tony said.

"Ouch," said Aiden, "unfortunate name. He's always walking the hall with an instrument case, though. Pretty much anyone lugging one of those is just asking for it. See? It was *his* fault. He should have just put the case down and no one would have gotten hurt. In a way, *I'm* the victim—no, those *eggs* are the poor freakin' victims."

"Little babies didn't even have a chance," Tony said, and coughed, choking on some phlegm.

I'm losing respect for myself *right now. Every minute I spend with these guys is just...*

The girl hadn't thrown anything, but Maggie still felt bad. She couldn't help imagining the boy's father after he found the egg remains, perhaps noticing them on his way to work the next day. Since egging was almost always an expression of the young, it would undoubtedly remind the man—or shamefully illustrate to him—his son's less-than-impressive social standing at school.

Okay nobody died *Maggie. You're probably taking it worse*

23

than the people who got hit will. Relax.

She tried not thinking about it and looked up to see that the stars were especially bright that night. Around her the sky seemed to grow as the trees thinned out at the top of the hill.

"Hey," Aiden said, pinching Stephanie's bottom. "Wanna tell you somethin'. Not in front of these guys though. Come over here with me?" He tipped his head in the direction of one of the few trees around.

Stephanie turned to Maggie and rolled her eyes as she walked off.

Ah crap, Maggie thought, realizing that she was about to be left alone with Tony Bardou. She opened her mouth to say something, hoping to stall them, but couldn't think of anything quick enough that made sense. Aiden and Stephanie were already becoming shadows as they approached the base of a tall pine.

You dork—of course *this is what they wanted to do. "We're just gonna walk around." Okay! I like walking! Awesome.*

"Aaand here we are," Tony said, staring at Maggie. "So. What kind of stuff you into?"

Maggie looked around nervously. "Stuff? You mean like hobbies or drugs?"

6

Tony smiled, making an effort to look cooler than he had all night. "Either," he said.

"Well." Maggie paused, then added, "I don't do drugs—I don't even drink yet—but I like reading, and I draw a lot."

Tony nodded. "Exciting."

"Thanks."

After a sigh, he looked over at the pine. "They're *so* gonna suck face."

Maggie cringed.

"And Stephanie has braces," Tony continued, "which means Aiden's gonna get some of her dinner tonight. You like leftovers?" The boy chuckled.

Maggie shook her head, hoping that she wasn't going to

have to pepper-spray him at some point. She seriously considered leaving, and then said, "Oh crap." Turning, she looked back down the hill.

"What? You hear something?"

"No, but we can't—" She glanced around. "How the heck are we getting home?"

"Um, *walking*?"

"Through the *woods*?" Maggie pointed at the pine tree. "He just egged a house on a dead-end street."

Tony looked up the hill and then nodded. "Oh. You mean those people'll probably be out front looking—"

"Yeah."

"We could walk behind some houses."

"Down the hill? And just hope no one's on their porch?"

"Well what the hell do you *want* to do?" Tony said. "Fly? Just relax. We'll hang out here until everyone's asleep and then cruise on back. You know, you're really high-strung."

And she was. He wasn't getting an argument there. Maggie knew she thought too much, was thin-skinned, and probably displayed a handful of other neurotic symptoms, but the last thing she wanted to do was stand around in the middle of the night and get diagnosed by Tony Bardou. He had his own damn problems.

"Maybe they aren't tonguin'," Tony said.

Maggie turned to see where the boy was looking. He was facing the tall pine again, and she could see something by its base, where the long dark branches fanned out to cover the ground. It was Stephanie. She was crouched down and waving, though not in a greeting. She was motioning for them to stay low. Maggie stooped and scanned the street.

"The cops?" Tony asked.

"Don't know. I'm going to see."

"That's stupid. I'm not movin'."

Ignoring him, Maggie hunched over and started across the street. But before she could reach the other side, Stephanie raised both hands and motioned for her to stop. She pointed to the ground and Maggie knelt—though the girl wasn't going to stay there in no-man's-land between the road and the only tree around. If a police car came over the hill, she'd be lit up like a billboard. Maggie crawled on all fours to the base of the tree, despite Stephanie's protests.

"*What?*" she asked, tucking under one of the pine's limbs.

"I told you to stay there!" Stephanie whisper-shouted.

"Not out in the open," Maggie answered.

Stephanie grunted and turned back toward the tree. "There's someone over there—just shut up for now."

Moving slowly, Maggie scooted around the pine to look for herself. On the other side was a small ranch house lined by two rows of overgrown shrubs. Beside it were a sandbox and a few big wheels under another tree.

"Are they *inside*?" she whispered, but Stephanie didn't answer. "I don't see any—" But she *did* see something; something that moved at the base of that tree. The pitch-black shape she had dismissed as only the trunk was something more. It looked like a man standing there, at least as tall as her, his jacket flipping out below the waist as he knelt. Maggie's heart skipped when she realized she had been wrong again. They weren't all toys at the base of the tree. With her pulse thumping in her ears, she looked more closely at the shadows beneath and saw the silhouette of a knee, and then a foot. The dark figure was kneeling over a body.

7

Maggie reached for her phone, but her hand stopped before sliding into the pocket. The screen would be way too bright. She couldn't turn it on there.

Call the police somewhere else.

Holding her breath, she looked back at the stranger beneath the tree.

And please, no one get a text right now.

A light flashed under the man, and immediately Maggie thought, *Cell phone?* But it was too intense and too brief. It was more like a bulb burning out, spending all its energy in one final declaration before dying. In that flicker of light, she saw a pale face and black hair. The figure on the ground beside him was a woman.

Get out and call for help. Now. *Slowly, but now.*

Turtling up like never before, Maggie shrank within herself and merged with the branches. Quietly she shuffled her feet backward, hoping to slide any dead twigs out of the way.

"There's no one here!"

It was Tony, shouting from across the street.

Idiot.

"You guys hear me?" he yelled again.

The pine tree beside Maggie shook.

"Outta this shit!" Aiden blurted out, as he swatted branches away and sprinted across the grass.

Stephanie pushed up from the ground, glanced from Maggie to the figures under the tree, and then ran.

"Wait," Maggie began, and then froze. She moved her eyes rather than her head to see if she had gone unnoticed. She hadn't. The stranger was only ten yards away and quickly striding toward her.

As Maggie crab-walked backward, she bent a branch with her head and it slipped past, rebounding into her face. Temporarily blinded by pine needles, the girl rolled over and scrambled to her feet. Through pained, squinted eyes she saw Aiden, Tony, and Stephanie disappearing down the hill.

"We're leaving!" Maggie cried out as she ran. "They were just egging houses—and we didn't even *hit* yours!" She hoped the stranger was buying her naïveté and didn't know that she had actually seen the woman beneath him. But he wasn't slowing.

If she couldn't lose her pursuer, she at least wanted to keep him in her sights. When the girl made it to the road, she turned around to face him.

"Stop! Back up!" Maggie yelled, digging into her bag for the pepper spray.

But he continued walking toward her, staring and saying nothing. The collar of what looked like a peacoat flipped up with the wind and partially covered his face.

"I said stop damn it!" Maggie shouted again, hoping someone in a nearby house would hear. "Help! Police!" She raised the small canister and released a blast of spray. It struck the stranger in the chest, but only rose to his neck before he pulled the can from her hand and threw it to the side.

She had been too close. Maggie had waited too long.

But why isn't it hurting *you?* she thought. *I didn't hit your eyes, but—*

Instantly the girl's own eyes closed and began to water. Tears ran down her cheeks as some of the fine potent mist drifted back toward her.

But the man didn't even blink. With a chest full of spray, he only stared.

Maggie tried once more to flee. She whirled around, but her messenger bag was snagged before she could take a step. Her fear turning to panic, she shrugged off her bag only to have her extended hand snatched and pulled back. Maggie stumbled off balance in the stranger's cold, strong grip. He then spun her around and stared at her with eyes wide.

He was young, perhaps in his mid-twenties, but his skin seemed thin and was sickly in tone. Dark circles framed his eyes and his black hair stood out in pointed clusters. Still he didn't speak. Instead, there was a sharp intake of air, as if he had been underwater and just breached the surface. Grasping her arm, the young man drew Maggie close. His eyebrows knit together as he took in her features. A smile touched the corners of his mouth.

But Maggie didn't see this; for her eyes had completely closed since the spray on his chest was so near.

"Let go!" she yelled, then coughed, the chemicals entering her lungs and setting them on fire. "Help! How can you—"

Stop talking! she thought, and with a quick, frantic motion she pulled her knee up.

She hit him hard, either in the upper thigh or in the most tender of places, but his grip never faltered. Maggie willed her eyes to open, hoping to see some pain register on his face, but there was none. Still the young man leaned in close, with an expression almost of wonder. Of his own accord he released her arm and placed his hand behind her head. It was cold, almost freezing there at the base of her skull. But it couldn't be his hand; no human hand—no matter how cold—would emit such a biting chill.

Maggie's head throbbed, and someone shouted.

"Hey!"

She could hear the voice, but it was either far away or her hearing had diminished.

"You two okay?"

The stranger removed his hand from her head.

"I said are you guys all right? You need help?" It was a man's voice.

"Help," Maggie said softly. She turned to see joggers, a man and a woman, approaching. "Help!" she said with more strength. "Call the police."

8

"You hurt? Is he bothering you?" The male jogger ran up to them and stopped a few yards off. "Hey buddy back up will you? Is he hurting you Miss?"

"Yes," Maggie said. "I don't know him and I want to get away."

The young man in the peacoat released Maggie's hand and stepped back.

"Jill call the police," the jogger said. "And take this guy's picture. Hey pal nobody wants any trouble here. We're all just gonna leave each other alone. Does that sound good?"

The young man didn't answer, but he did continue stepping back. He turned to Maggie and she saw his face lighten. It wasn't a smile, but some of the tension left his features. Faint lines disappeared from his brow and his head tilted slightly.

"Yeah hi, I'm on Dodson Street," Jill said into her phone. "Can you send someone out here? There's a—"

Maggie moved behind the male jogger and rubbed her neck. Quietly she said, "There's a woman under the tree over there."

The jogger motioned for Jill to back away. With his eyes still on the young man, he asked Maggie, "He have a weapon?"

"I haven't seen any yet."

"The police'll be here in a minute," he said, "and everything will be cool, all right?"

This time the young man *did* smile—at Maggie, she thought—then he turned and walked into an open field near the woods.

"I'll call you back." Jill hung up, switched to camera, and the digital sound effect of an aperture closing cycled again and again. "Damn it. I had to call them first though."

"Yeah you did." The man tapped Maggie on the shoulder and turned away from the field. He then signaled for Jill to follow, and said, "Let's go find a house nearby where we can sit for a bit hunh?"

9

"Six dogs," the big officer said, making a left-hand turn onto Oak Street.

Maggie had nicknamed the man Bear in her own mind because he was enormous and had a mustache that looked like a rolled-up carpet.

"I been there three years, maybe four now I suppose. Nice place but come on. It's gotta be six or seven dogs I've found, me and the wife, roamin' around our front and stuff."

"That *is* a lot," his partner, Brickman, said. Maggie knew this officer's name because she'd heard it enough at the station. It had stuck because he was unremarkable enough for no other nickname to take its place. "That's more dogs than one man should handle in that time."

"It's ridiculous." Bear glanced in the rearview mirror at Maggie, not because she drew his attention, but more out of habit whenever there was a passenger in the backseat. "Look, my point is it's a lot of dogs and I'm not even getting *paid*. That'd be something. If I had ten bucks a dog…" He smiled. "And it happened again."

"Another dog?" Brickman asked.

Bear nodded.

"Recently?"

"Yesterday," Bear said, like he'd been through a war. "On my day off of course."

"Obviously."

"So," Bear continued, "I'm checkin' out the window on my front door like I do four hundred times a day because I live in a constant state of code red—"

"Cops, baby."

Bear shook his head. "Nah, that's just me. I'm paranoid. So I see this yellow lab or a golden mix—they're all looking the same to me now, everyone has a yellow lab or a golden—but anyway, it's cruising up the hill to my house. And there's not a soul in sight."

"Of course. Free range," Brickman added.

Maggie looked down as she smirked.

"Free range, roamin' the neighborhood, collecting ticks for us—it was very nice of him—but no one around." Bear sighed louder than necessary. "So I'm thinkin' here we go. I walk outside and it took me thirty minutes to get this skittish thing over to me before I could tell he had no tags on his collar."

"Oh perfect. It's getting better. But hey, you're the size of a squad car—you'd scare a horse. You couldn't send your little wife over? She's sweeter than candy. She'd get the thing eatin' out of her hand in a minute."

"Sure, but what if it takes her hand *off*? You don't know what a dog's got in its head."

Brickman shrugged.

"So there I am," Bear continued, "up and down the neighborhood we go, every damn walker, jogger, construction guy, I'm askin', 'Have you seen this dog? You know whose this is?' Luckily it was following me. But we must have done close to two miles. Meanwhile this thing's running through the woods, and it had to have jumped in the lake at one point because it came back *soaked*." Both men laughed. "Looked like a drowned rat. With sticks and leaves all tied up on it. I didn't know if it was gonna make it. It was catchin' Lyme disease, Ebola, rickets—whatever the hell was out there. Anyway, we finally get back and I call animal control."

"Hey you tried."

"No shit." Bear looked in the rearview at Maggie. "Excuse me dear. But yeah, they pick him up, turn the corner, and then a minivan comes at me from the other direction. 'Have you seen my dog?'"

The two officers shared another laugh, and Bear mimicked cinching a noose around his neck.

Despite what had happened to her that night—the close encounter with the deranged stranger, the interview at the station—Maggie had to laugh. Bear and Brickman had been in charge of the case all evening, and they'd been nothing but nice. The two had spoken to her, the joggers, and the three other kids, for more than two and a half hours, taping everything and taking notes.

The young man in the peacoat hadn't yet been found; but luckily, the woman under the tree was not severely injured. Her name was Sherry Bradley. She had been cleaning the grill on her back porch when the stranger assaulted her. By the time she was discovered, she had suffered a few scrapes and bruises, but more seriously, was unconscious. The woman remained this way during transport to Hickins Hospital, where she still lay in a comatose state.

Of all the minors interviewed, Maggie was the only one whose family couldn't be reached at home. But this didn't surprise her. True, it was the wee hours of the morning, but her father never answered the phone anyway. And even if he had known she was out, chances were he wouldn't have been overly concerned.

Maggie caught Officer Bear's eyes in the mirror again. They were kind eyes, and she could tell he had seen this situation before: no one to contact by phone, having to escort a youth back to his or her house. He knew what he was dealing with, and Maggie couldn't help but feel embarrassed by it.

"It's just up ahead, right Ms. Muntin?" he asked, motioning through the windshield to the right.

"Yep," Maggie said, quickly looking down.

"And listen now," Officer Brickman said, looking over his shoulder. "We'll keep our eyes peeled for that creep, but you and your friends let us know if he pokes his head up anywhere too. Okay?"

"Okay."

"It'll be a team thing."

The patrol car rolled to a stop. Officer Bear looked over his right shoulder and said, "I'll let you out honey, it's locked on the inside."

10

Mr. Muntin surprised Maggie, Bear, and Brickman by answering the door quickly. Judging by his bag-ridden, blinking eyes, Maggie figured he hadn't made it to bed, and had been on the couch a few feet away, watching TV.

Inside, Bear and Brickman described the previous night's events to him. Mr. Muntin conveyed a reasonable facsimile of concern, even managing small talk where appropriate.

When Officer Bear noticed Maggie inching away, he offered her his card. The girl smiled and nodded, then crept up the stairs while the three men spoke further.

Since her phone's battery had died hours before, the time on her nightstand clock was a surprise: 4:30 a.m.

"Ugh," she moaned. "So freakin' tired and no time. Like I

could sleep anyway." But she wanted to; the girl was beyond exhausted. She felt light-headed and her eyes burned, but too much was happening; there were too many things to think about.

She rubbed her left eye with her palm. It had been throbbing since the police picked her up.

You gotta work on your pepper-spray skills girl. The creep is fine and my *eye is messed up? That's about right.*

Half-tripping on a slipper, she shuffled over to the window and looked down at the empty police car. Holding her breath, she could still hear the voices downstairs. It was probably the longest conversation her father had had with other human beings in months.

She leaned her forehead on the window and it squeaked across the glass. Ignoring the oil smear, Maggie scanned the street and surrounding neighborhood. The sky was no longer black since the sun was already on its way. The girl didn't see anyone outside, no lurkers in the bushes or any shadows out of place, but that didn't ease the tension.

Attempting to be quiet, Maggie left her bedroom on light feet, crossed the hall, and entered the spare room at the back of the house. There, she slid a box out from under the room's only window and stepped close. A small lawn, a tall fence, and the neighbors' houses. No shadows, and no eyes staring back.

Still not sleeping. I mean this is good *but come on. Gonna have to do something.*

After walking back to her room, Maggie placed her sketch pad on the floor and was about to drop the day's mail there as well, when she saw the return address of the Salem District Court.

Oh my gosh. Tell me this is it. It took long enough.

The girl opened the envelope to find a copy of her approval for emancipation.

The process had taken longer than eight months and required more effort than almost anything she had done in her life. In order to appeal correctly, Maggie had needed her father's written consent (a small thing on his part, but she was amazed he lifted a pen to do it), she had to file the petition, forward proof of a freelance income (to show she could support herself), attend the preliminary meeting, and finally the drawn-out, intimidating, uncomfortable court hearing. So much grown-up stuff. So much stuff she didn't want to do.

I'm not gonna think about this right now though. Empty thoughts Maggie—you should be good at that. Empty head, empty thoughts. But my head's full of the stressed-out echoes of my life. Sounds like a band name. She let out a deep breath and her forearms tingled. *Clear your head. It's good though. This is good.*

A smile touched her lips, and she felt a little guilty for it.

Blank paper. Snow field.

The girl slipped out of her shoes and shrugged off her jacket. The bedsprings squeaked beneath her as she lay back. After another deep breath, she rubbed her left eye again. The ache was still there, and it had started to feel cold.

11

He couldn't get any closer. The stranger had found the police car that had picked up everyone on Dodson Street, but he couldn't approach. Now it was parked in front of a home marked number thirteen. And a light was on. He hadn't seen anyone; he got there too late for that. He wondered if the girl lived there. Maybe. But he couldn't get close. And the sun was on its way. That never helped.

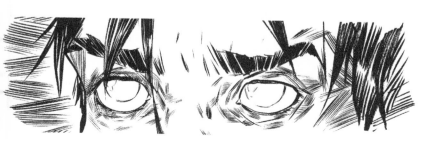

12

There had been a few very long blinks, but otherwise, Maggie never got anywhere close to sleep. She watched the minute hand inch around the clock, but that was it. At ten till five, she heard Bear and Brickman's car doors shut, the engine start, and then fade in the distance. At five thirty she stared at the ceiling. From six to six thirty, Maggie paced between the two upstairs windows twenty-seven times. She stopped only for fear of wearing through the floor and falling into the living room below. If that happened, the girl was sure she would come crashing down onto her father's lap and then *have* to talk to him. You couldn't get up off someone's lap amid crumbling plaster, exchange awkward glances, then walk off without a word. Nope. Maggie was pretty sure that wouldn't work. They would *have* to talk about something. So to avoid that, or lying in bed with wide-open eyes, she drew chipmunks.

Maggie didn't bother turning on the lamp. The sun's light already reflecting off the white ceiling was enough to draw by.

The super-powered chipmunk toy line was still in the early development stages, so rough sketches were all Looksee Toys would need for now. This was good because there was no way she was going to produce finished art before school; the inking and coloring would come later. In the next thirty minutes, Maggie loosely sketched a dozen variations of possible chipmunk butt kickers, each one in a slightly different style, with slightly different proportions and expressions. If the pieces she turned in were too similar, and the style or vision wasn't what the art directors had in mind, they would thank her for her time and try another artist. However, if she turned in a variety of options, chances were one might be close to what they were thinking and that direction could be pursued. This would allow her to stay on the job longer and hopefully earn more. The key was simply reading the editor's or art director's mind. Which was impossible. And what made things even more interesting was when Maggie realized that she wasn't the only one with trouble expressing herself. It seemed that artist types in general were horrible. Many editors thought comments like "let's try another pass. This time make him more present, more there" were helpful. She had heard things like "more lively proportions," "hair that is less angry," and "more details but fewer lines" before. This was the kind of stuff that scrambled brains. Often, the key to freelancing was to bite her tongue, submit art over and over, and meet her deadlines.

Once a few drawings were complete, she took photos of the chipmunks with her phone, adjusted the levels so that the line art was clear and sharp, and sent them in.

A little after seven o'clock, Maggie spritzed her bonsai on the windowsill and went downstairs to the kitchen. She crept past her father, who was asleep on the couch, filled a small bowl with cereal, and quietly took it upstairs. After breakfast, she brushed her teeth, used the bathroom, towel bathed (unable to muster the resolve for a shower), and threw on acceptable clothes for the day. These would be something she felt comfortable in, hadn't worn in a few weeks, and that didn't have holes yet. Sadly, the pickings were getting slim.

She looked quickly in the mirror.

Yep. A weak chin and electrical-tape eyebrows. Check and check. It's still me. A supermodel didn't steal my body last night—not even a dumpy *model.*

She smiled in spite of herself.

At seven twenty, Maggie started her walk to school. She made it before the first bell at eight fifteen.

And school was school.

Classes passed slowly.

Very.

She managed to check her email in fourth-period study hall and saw that chipmunks C and G had been approved for finished pencils.

Sweet. That'll be some *money. And I liked C too. Tell me these guys have good taste.* But she stopped herself before thinking it would be an easy job.

Fighting the urge to start penciling immediately, Maggie slid her phone back into her bag and started on her pre-calculus homework instead. It made her long for her geometry days, which had been little better than miserable.

It wasn't long before her mind drifted from math to the emancipation documents in her room.

Wait, do I need to forward anything?

Two weeks ago, Maggie had received an email from the

Department of Educational Services at Gilligan High School in Marblehead, New Hampshire. Though she had lived in Connecticut all her life, she had always dreamed of moving farther north, and the town where the school resided was beautiful. With her independence finally granted, she was getting close. The email had notified her that "State documents have been received." At the time she had no idea what that meant, but didn't want to follow up for fear of confusing the transfer process. Now she knew what it referred to. The required documents must have been forwarded automatically.

But just in case, Maggie made a note to email the school's administration office and see if any additional documents were needed. With a little luck, she could transfer before Gilligan High's spring break.

Now all I need are some wheels. Maggie covered a smile with her hand. *My gosh I need to do so much damn stuff. Compartmentalize, right? Small pieces. Bite-sized chunks. Can you have a nervous breakdown at seventeen?* She shook her head. *Drama queen. Let's keep it calm Maggs. Baby steps.*

The bell rang, signaling the end the period and the beginning of lunch.

Argh, I didn't pack food. Maybe Dad did.

It was supposed to be a joke, but unfortunately it felt nothing like one.

Since study hall was in the cafeteria, Maggie left her bag on the table and headed for the vending machines. Looking down as she pulled out her bunny-shaped coin purse, she bumped into someone.

"Slow down, rushie," a boy named Tom Vilpatrick said over his shoulder. "There's plenty of crap food for—" His face soured before he finished the sentence. "What's wrong with your *eye*?"

Maggie's heart sank. "What do you mean?"

"Like your hair isn't freaky enough. Is that a contact?"

"No, I don't wear 'em. What are you looking at?"

The boy pointed up at her face. "Your pupil's like a creepy white."

13

Maggie ran to the restroom, positive that Tom was full of it. Her eye *felt* okay, at least for the moment, and she could see fine. It was messed up a bit last night—or that morning, too—but she could still see.

"Shit," she said, her mouth falling open and her face inches from the mirror.

Her left pupil was nearly white—a very light blue-gray. It could still be seen, but barely.

After blinking several times, Maggie covered her right eye and focused with the left, both near and far. Everything seemed okay. The girl looked closer in the mirror to see if she had officially lost her mind and just forgot about putting in a contact lens.

Study hall. Maybe I fell asleep and some really messed-up, quiet ninja-freak snuck one in. That's the dumbest thing I've ever—

"There's no ring around it or line though," she said out loud.

A toilet flushed behind her.

Sarah Pickling, a six-foot-two sophomore, stepped out of a stall and stared at Maggie. "People say you talk to yourself a lot. They're right. You really shouldn't do that. Not so much at least, or in public." The girl turned and pulled open the restroom door to leave.

Maggie shook her head and turned back to the mirror. "Says the girl who doesn't wash her hands," she mumbled. "I'm taking advice from *you*?"

She sighed and thought, *But there's no ring for the contact. And I'd still be able to see the little black dot in the middle of my eye. The iris? Whatever it is. I couldn't see at all if that was covered up. But I can see* fine *damn it. Tell me my eye's not dying.*

There was an optometrist two miles from school near the center of town. After classes ended, Maggie speed-walked there in record time. She waited an hour and fifteen minutes to speak with Dr. Amalla Rijni, and thanked the woman for seeing her without an appointment. But she still left with concerns. Dr. Rijni had checked Maggie's eye inside and out, and said that her vision was fine; that both her eye movements and coordination were normal. The doctor found no signs of cataracts on her lens or glaucoma on the optic nerve. But still something was wrong. The woman recommended visiting an ophthalmologist for further study. Maggie thanked her and walked home a little frightened and very close to tears.

But I didn't get hurt. There wasn't an injury.

And she knew what those felt like. When she was seven and a half, she had been hit in the eye with a badminton birdie—not the coolest of accidents, but it counted. Her partner serving had taken a bit too long, and she thought that turning around to see why was a good idea. It wasn't. The shuttlecock hit her eye at full speed from a few feet away. Maggie collapsed to the ground and her eye immediately filled with blood. She went blind instantly and spent the next five days in the hospital while the blood diminished and drained. It hurt. A lot. Though after a few weeks, everything did return to normal.

With this faded pupil, there was no pain, no injury she could point to. She appreciated the clean bill of health so far, but not knowing the cause was eating away at her.

The creep in the peacoat...he—

She wasn't sure what he did. There was no trauma. He hadn't struck her. He only held the back of her head for a moment, though when he did, Maggie remembered she had felt cold.

A stinging cold. In my head and *my eye.*

It *seemed* right, it added up in a way, yet it made her feel worse.

Quickly she spun around. A nearly overwhelming feeling of loneliness and vulnerability washed over her. There was a boy riding the opposite way on a BMX bike, but no one else was around. Even so, Maggie closed her left eye; she was embarrassed by it, and untrusting. She walked home feeling that a bit of herself had been taken, that she had been used. But what was worse was the feeling that the unknown, unfound creep that did it had left a part of him with her.

14

Over the next two days her eye behaved itself. Other than remaining a freaky, dead-fish, ghostly white, there wasn't any discomfort or further changes.

It did take a while, but her father eventually noticed it and asked, "What happened to your eye?"

Fibbing, Maggie answered that it was a contact, and they left it at that. After the brief interaction, she returned to her room and felt a strange appreciation that the man had at least asked.

Kind of a sad state of affairs when that's a positive, she thought. *"At least he said something"? That's like saying at least I have a pulse. How low a bar can you set Maggs? Apparently really low.*

To help take her mind off both the eye and Cold-fingers-Mcpeacoat, she drew more chipmunks. When the first batch of tight pencils was approved, she inked each figure and then colored them on her old laptop. After a few coloring corrections, Looksee Toys said they were happy with the final images and began processing an invoice for direct deposit into her account.

Throughout the job (while waiting for either approval or comments), Maggie had monitored the sale status of three RVs online. The girl had bookmarked these in her favorites a few months before and pulled up the sales pages of each religiously, perhaps compulsively: definitely compulsively. So much so that she hoped there wasn't a hit counter tracking computer IPs showing how OCD she was; flagging compulsive clickers as unfit for sale. Luckily she never got banned, but Maggie *did* watch two of the RVs get nabbed up before her eyes. This wasn't good news, but the girl didn't get upset because both of them had been priced a bit high. Maybe totally legitimate value-wise, but more than she could afford. That left the least expensive, longest-listed, and oldest RV still available. It didn't sound *too* appealing, but Maggie decided it was worth a look. The seller, Ernest Peppersnach (her new favorite name), lived only three miles from school. The girl called him and asked if they could meet before dinner, making sure to give herself enough time to get there on foot after classes. He agreed with a pleasant voice shaped by a thick Yankee accent. Maggie could tell by his tone that he was either slightly suspicious of a call by such a young woman, or was impressed by it.

It turned out he *was* impressed, though that might have been because she had made it all the way up the driveway to his house. The young lady was breathing hard, with sweat on her brow, when she found the man standing outside his garage.

"You know," Ernest said, scratching his short gray beard, "most people just drive up."

Maggie paused a moment and looked at him. She figured that her youth and the fact that she was walking would have made things clear. "Well, that's why I'm here today sir."

"You don't have a car and you want to buy an RV?" he said, casually grasping the straps of his overalls.

"I'm thinking about it."

The man nodded in silence. After a bit, he said, "You wanna sit down? You look a little worse for wear. Not sure if you'll make it

over to the vehicle."

A comedian, she thought. The girl smiled. She had a soft spot for the dry Yankee humor, and so did Mr. Peppersnach apparently, for he was smiling at his own joke.

"I got a little left in me," Maggie said.

"Some ice water? A cold towel?" Now his eyes were smiling, too.

"I'll be fine, thanks. How about just half price for your listing?"

The man's eyebrows went up and he looked around. "Right to business hunh? And right for my throat it seems." He turned back to Maggie and looked her over from head to toe. "I better keep my eye on you."

Her thoughts turned to her own eye, and she was thankful that it hadn't been brought up yet. "Oh I'm pretty harmless," she said, "if I get good deals."

Ernest rolled his eyes. "Listen to her. I already offered you water."

The man turned and headed toward his house, and Maggie followed. When the driveway leveled off, she could see the RV beneath a tarp in a copse of trees.

"The sheet's to keep the pine sap off—you'll thank me for that if you buy it. But I'm not gonna lie, she needs a bit of work. There's some engine trouble, she's down two tires, and there's a family of raccoons in it now so don't raise yer voice."

Maggie stared at the man.

Casually he said, "Just kidding." He then turned to her

with his eyes wide, shook his head, and put a finger to his lips.

Maggie found herself giggling, though she still wasn't sure about the raccoons. "This is the highlight of your day isn't it? Grossing out a young lady."

"Man's gotta have his hobbies."

"Well you're not sweetenin' the deal any. How much were you paying me to take that thing?"

Smiling, Ernest pulled off the tarp. "Might've been tryin' to scare you off with a few of those comments. I've been known to take some liberties with the truth, so it's told." The man tapped the side of the vehicle. "But as you can see, the ol' lady's doin' all right."

Maggie crouched to find that all four tires were present and accounted for. She stood and walked over to one of its tinted windows. "I don't hear any clawing inside."

"Then they must be out."

"In that case it might be a good time for me to take a peek."

"As you wish," Ernest said. He took the keys from his chest pocket. "I'll wait out front here while you just poke around, how's that?"

"Fine thanks." Maggie appreciated the space.

Nice of him to offer. I was gonna bring that up, but how? "Hey old fella, I don't trust your looks. You mind staying outside your own RV?"

Shouldn't matter though. Safety rule number 468: don't let awkwardness prevent you from protecting yourself. Ever. But

thanks Mr. Peppersnach—as long as there's not a dead body in here.
Maggie turned the key and opened the door.

15

There were no animals chewing the wires or humping on the seats, but the smell... To say that Mr. Peppersnach was a smoker would have been an understatement. Maggie recognized the strong and distinctive odor of pipe smoke before holding her breath and stepping inside. As fast as she was able, the girl slid open three windows on the left side of the vehicle and one on the right rear. By the time she made it to the front, she was already seeing stars. After popping open the front doors, Maggie stuck her head out and gasped for breath.

Mr. Peppersnach looked amused.

"You wouldn't happen to be a *smoker* would you?" she asked.

The man laughed and pinched his index finger and thumb together, indicating a little.

"I'm gonna need a *mask* to check the rest of this out," Maggie said, then disappeared inside. The interior looked to be in good shape, however. There was a dark spot on the counter where a hot pan might have been set, and two patches stitched on the couch in the rear, but everything else was minor. The mileage was good, too. It had sixty-four thousand miles on it, which was by no means a lot for an RV more than eighteen years old.

She closed the windows and doors, then exited the vehicle. "That smell is *never* coming out of my hair."

"You're layin' it on a little thick ain'tcha?"

"*I'm* laying it on thick? Those *fumes* were thick. You could break that RV up, put it in a pipe, and never have to buy tobacco again."

Ernest smiled. "You sound like my late wife."

Maggie didn't feel like being sassy after that remark, so she just turned back to the vehicle.

"I can tell you're pretty excited about it," the man said. "I'm guessing you'll take it?"

The girl smirked. "I think I know why it's still for sale."

"Well I *did* have three or four folks come through already, takin' a peek. They might not have made it out actually. Bump into anyone?"

"Nope, didn't see them. How 'bout this though, would you take eight thousand for it?"

Mr. Peppersnach's smile disappeared. He paused a moment and then asked, "Is this a stickup?"

Trying to hide a smile, Maggie looked away.

"Am I surrounded? Look, I don't want any trouble." The man took a stubby pipe from his pocket and began packing tobacco in the chamber. "Honestly, it's a good vehicle. In good shape, with not a lot of miles on her. 'Course, she smells like holy hell 'cause o' this." He put the pipe to his lips. "But I'll tell you what. I'll take two thousand off what I listed her for."

"Mr. Peppersnach—I love your name by the way—it's gonna cost me that much to get it *deodorized*."

"The heck you say!"

"How about four thousand under listing and I write a check for you today."

"Wow," the man said. "Look at you. Well, I won't ask you where you got the money."

"Drawing. I earned it," she said, a bit more coldly than intended. Maggie worked hard, and always resented it when people implied that things had come easily.

"I'm sure you did," Ernest said. "And I didn't mean anything by it. You've impressed me quite a bit today, even though I'm bein' a little silly."

Maggie looked down and nodded.

"How 'bout this now: *three* thousand less, and did you notice the little ramp on the back bumper?"

"Hmm? No."

"Well, it's for that." Ernest pointed into his open garage at a Honda Ruckus parked against the far wall.

"Is that a scooter?"

"It is. Ever ride one?"

"Nope."

"Want to?"

Maggie thought about the RV—the price, the miles, the condition—then she looked at the white scooter in the garage. "Okay."

65

16

Maggie liked the scooter.

Her white locks bounced wildly as she did figure eights on the man's driveway. She would have to order a helmet, though, making sure it was large enough to hold her silvery mane.

Buying the RV wasn't a difficult choice. The lower price not only allowed her to write a check she could cover, but also left her with a few thousand for the things that might lie ahead. A name for the vehicle had even come to her as she was leaving the property. She would dub it *Soggy Biscuits*, in honor of her favorite comic strip. In that weekly series, the two French bulldogs would only eat biscuits that had been broken in half and soaked in water for no less than a minute. They found this made chewing and swallowing far less of a chore (a Frenchie's tolerance for such things was extremely low), especially on those annoyingly dry days. Plus, Maggie thought the name sounded cute, almost like the name of a vessel. She loved the idea of the RV as her boat.

After Mr. Peppersnach signed over the vehicle's title, Maggie folded it and put it in the back of her sketchbook. She then emailed herself a note with a reminder to apply for one in her own name at the clerk's office.

Piloting the small craft, the girl carefully navigated down the streets and around the corners to its first stop, the Super Saveprice Co. There, she left the RV at the far end of the parking lot where there were fewer vehicles and it was easier to maneuver. Maggie refused to think of this as a cop-out because it *was* her maiden voyage.

At the superstore, she bought water (because she drank like a fish) and a case of baking soda (because the RV still smelled like a forest after a fire). The girl then drove all the way home with the windows open and the curtains flapping against the walls. As she pulled up in front of her house, she saw her father come to the window. The RV purchase was a surprise to him, since the girl had never actually brought it up. Mr. Muntin stared at it suspiciously, backlit by the cold fluorescent lights in the kitchen.

When Maggie stepped out, she offered a wave, and it took a moment for the man either to register who it was, or to decide whether to return the gesture. He did wave, awkwardly, but then turned away.

"Not into RVs I guess," she said, petting the side of the vehicle. "It's all right *Soggy*. He doesn't know what he's missing. But right now, baby needs a little tender loving care."

Hopping back into *Soggy Biscuits*, Maggie cut open the case of baking soda, took out the first of twenty boxes, and dumped it on the driver's seat. The second box she poured on the passenger's side; the third, on the carpet that led to the back; while the rest was scattered on the couches, in the cabinets, under the seats, all over the bathroom, and then the curtains (which she would take down and wash at some point).

Maggie grinned as she drew her finger across the powder on the bathroom counter and wiped some of it under her nose. She then leaned in closer to the mirror and noticed the mounds of baking soda in the shower and on the carpet behind her. With hooded eyes and a slack jaw, she mumbled at her reflection, "Bitch I don't have a drug problem!" When she got to the *p* in *problem*, the powder on her lip shot up her nose and onto the mirror. Coughing uncontrollably, Maggie tried to wipe the rest of it off her face.

Totally normal. And I wonder why people think I'm nuts.

She decided to keep the windows and side door cracked for the night, but closed all the screens. On her way up to the house, with her path lit by the half-moon, Maggie paused and looked back at *Soggy Biscuits*. She stared at the RV, letting what it represented sink in.

Crickets, both far and near, chirped around her.

Though she was unsure of what lay ahead and absolutely nervous, Maggie smiled, because within her there was also a sense of contentment. For despite all the unknowns, those vague and dark shapes, through her own will, Maggie had found a little light.

17

A dog barked on every street he walked. Sometimes two or more howled out to the young man from behind closed windows or locked fences. They didn't care much for him, and the cats he encountered just stared. Most peered out from either the first or second floor of a home, yet one kitten gazed at him from outside, neither running away nor approaching. This little black-and-gray rogue simply watched the young man while sitting beside the carcass of half a mouse; the grisly remains of her nightly plunder.

Though he made an effort not to, he swallowed almost continuously as he walked, his throat clicking each time he did. It was dry, it always was, but that wasn't the extent of his problems. His body, his form, wasn't functioning as it should, as he was used to. He walked with unsteady legs, not quite stumbling, but as though they were half-asleep, lumbering a bit as he moved.

Rubbing a hand across his brow, he collected some of the dew that began to blanket the night. But his skin there wasn't supple; it hadn't absorbed any of the moisture around. Instead, it shifted reluctantly in one rigid mass.

He would need to find someone before long, or some*thing*, perhaps one of the cats that didn't seem to mind his presence; maybe something asleep. But that was far too rare a thing to hope for. It came down to access; that was everything.

The young man walked up and down the streets just outside of town, not yet pursuing a destination, only tolerating this nagging, continuous need. His skin tingled and his hair moved subtly toward the faint current he could feel emanating from each house. Objects, wiring, people, animals—all unseen, but easily felt and assessed.

At the corner of Wakefield Drive and Henderson Avenue, the stranger paused to let a pickup truck pass, its knobbed tires hissing along the damp asphalt. After following Henderson east for two blocks, he found what he needed. Stopping short, the young man's left leg faltered, nearly buckling beneath him. With a little effort, it soon straightened as he took in what was before him.

Less than twenty yards away, a man with glasses stood beside a Jeep. That man began speaking into his cell phone as rain started to fall.

"—don't care if he has to leave early," the man said, "no one wants him there *anyway*. *You've* met the guy. Ten minutes with him and you're lookin' for a door—or a bridge. Just have him drive it over *now* please. Yeah, tell him Aaron needs the car now. It's starting to come down."

The young man approached. He watched as Aaron tried to wipe his glasses with one hand while holding his phone in the other. Aaron then tried the door handle in front of him without success. It was only when he walked around to the other side that he noticed the silhouette near him.

"Can I help—" the man started to say. But that was all he

managed before being struck in the face.

The stranger pushed his forearm against Aaron's nose and tore the phone from the man's grasp.

"Hey, back up!" Aaron shouted, shoving away from the Jeep.

The cell phone sparked in the stranger's hand. A small flash of electricity skipped along his finger and entered his wrist. Aaron looked up in time to see that bolt leap from the young man's right eye and disperse in the rain.

The stranger tossed the phone into the street and lunged forward. He seized Aaron's shirt and dragged him away from the Jeep and down the sidewalk. He then threw the man behind a row of tall shrubs where none of the streetlights could reach.

"Dude—back off!" Aaron cried, blood running from his nose and over his mouth. "Help! Police! Hel—"

Without expression, the young man fell on him. There was no grimace or teeth bared. His calm face was deathly as he raised his left hand to cover Aaron's mouth and slid his right behind the man's head.

His glasses tumbled from his face and blood sprayed from the man's nose as he attempted to shout around his attacker's grip.

With quick, spidery fingers, the stranger tapped Aaron's skull and then walked those quivering digits along his neck. A purple glow rose from the man's head where he had been touched. The radiant color gathered into a sort of cluster of static that twisted and curled a few inches above him. This purple turned to shades of green as more of these luminescent bolts escaped from the back of Aaron's spine.

A car raced by less than fifteen feet away, but its driver was too concerned with the rain to notice any struggle in the shadows.

Aaron's eyes grew wide as he twisted at the hip, raised his shoulder, and freed the arm he had fallen on. With strength inspired more by terror than brawn, he swung his fist at the figure above him. The clenched hand flattened the young man's ear to his skull, but drew no other reaction. The stranger didn't strike back, but instead leaned forward and inhaled the gracefully moving green and now blue light. The young man's right hand circled around to Aaron's chest, moved up and down his sternum, then hovered above his stomach. Even more brilliant glows lifted from the clothing and continued changing form. In one moment it resembled static, and in another, a lethargic bolt of electricity that reshaped into what looked like a softly burning fog. The stranger raised his head as he tried to take in these elusive discharges. He bent to the left and reached with both hands as one escaped into the open air, while another met the trunk of a tree and sank within it.

Color faded from Aaron's eyes and his movements became slow. When his assailant leaned to the side for another glowing emanation, the man used what strength he had to arch his back and pitch him in that direction. And it worked. Teetering as though drunk, Aaron stood and pushed away from the shrubs. He moved clumsily between two parked cars, using their frames to steady himself. Yet even over the rain he could hear the footfalls of the stranger approaching. With his heart racing, Aaron stepped into the street, but made it only a few paces before he was struck by a van. His neck snapped, his hip dislocated, and his right femur shattered, tearing through muscle and tissue until the bone thrust out into the rain.

The young man in the peacoat remained in the shadows beside the shrubs. He watched the large vehicle skid to a stop twenty-two feet beyond the site of impact, noticed some movement in the cab, and looked on as it drove away.

18

The wolf stepped lightly across the lava field as smoke and cinders rose behind its cooling footprints to fade in the air.

Maggie erased a portion of the beast's back and loosely sketched a young girl riding with a thorned spear. She flipped the image over on her light box and tightened the penciled lines. The girl knew the light box was a bit of a crutch and probably would bring on early blindness, or at least a severe case of walleye at some point.

And eyestrain is exactly *what I need right now with the albino eye-thing I have going. Old habits die hard though.*

She knew it was important for an artist to be able to draw straight to the page, but a few years ago, Maggie had found that flipping sketches over allowed for liberties to be taken that improved them too much for her to want to stop. Redrawing anything backwards let her see the image fresh as if it were a new illustration, or one sketched by someone else. Because of this, it was easier to see the faults or weaknesses of the piece. And since the back of the page was clean, with no lines, Maggie could re-attack the drawing with confidence, knowing that no matter how much she tweaked the pose, limbs, proportions, or expressions, nothing would be lost, since all the original information was safe on the other side.

Once she had sketched a slightly tighter image on the back, Maggie would then erase the layout drawing on the front and get ready for a final pass of finished line art. Before picking up her mechanical pencil (usually a .03 for facial features and a .05 for the rest), Maggie would flip through an art book or scroll through some images online to change up her visuals. Staring at her own drawing for ten to twenty minutes at a time frequently would get it burned into her head and, as a result, mistakes could be too easily repeated, even with flipping the page. Ogling some brilliant art never failed to inspire, and it took her mind away from the images she had been creating. This was what was needed when she wanted to tackle the final drawing with confidence and fresh eyes. There were quite a few steps in this process, but over time Maggie had found that if she kept the first two stages loose and free, she could move at a good pace and find better shapes and lines overall. Unfortunately, to do all of this she needed an outlet and power; *plus* there was the whole cross-eyed blind thing, so it wasn't exactly a perfect system.

As she laid down more precise lines for the young girl's hair—keeping the strands in larger masses to imply the figure's movement—she added a small mask over the eyes with two horns that curled at the top.

I wonder if over-thinkers use a light box? The pencil stilled for a moment. *Laying out stuff, reediting, reworking, and* then *putting down the final drawing? A drawing that most viewers would think is the original. One that might come across as spontaneous, but is* totally *not.* Maggie smiled and shook her head. *It's how I live, too. I draw like I live. Maybe I should work on that. Acknowledging it's the first step right? And* all *artists are over-thinkers. Are you kidding me? We're barely functional closet cases.*

Checking the clock, she decided it was too late to break out her brush pen to ink the piece, so she just posted the penciled art on her social pages. As usual, typing, hashtagging, editing the text, and sharpening the image took nearly as much time as drawing it did, but building up her online following was important. It meant art sales, commissions, and, in the long run, hopefully would allow her to draw what she wanted to for a living, rather than what others told her to.

Once posted, Maggie checked her email and forwarded a message containing her medical history from her current doctor's office to Gilligan High School. It was one of the few remaining documents the school would need (she hoped) to allow her admittance.

Pausing for a minute, Maggie imagined a world where parents did this sort of thing for her, but she stopped almost immediately. It wasn't worth going down that road; dreaming about what different lives she would have if things were altered a bit in one way or another. Regrets and victimhood; Maggie had dabbled with them before, but found they only crippled and never uplifted.

Realizing there was no way she would be able to do a decent job of brushing her teeth without knowing how the lava-wolf-huntress-pixie-elf-thing was doing, she took out her phone. Seventy-three likes and two follows so far.

Nice. Good job Pixie-rider. Might have to record the inks.

She didn't bother looking at the comments yet; those could be checked in the morning. Especially the 20 percent of remarks that plagued every post, the "What tools are you using?" ones, even though she *always* listed her tools. Frustration was not the best aid to sleep, and she absolutely needed the rest, since tomorrow she was leaving home.

19

The rain coursing along Atwater Street pooled at the corner and flowed over a portion of the sidewalk. The young man walked through that inch-deep overflow until he reached Nicoli Lane. There, under the hum of a streetlamp, he stood staring at a motor home parked a few houses down. The vehicle sat dark and idle in front of house number thirteen: the girl's house.

He stared up at the home as he approached. The only illumination he could see was a cool blue light flickering without pattern in a first-floor window. He was familiar with these kinds of lights; he knew their source. Instead of approaching it, the stranger advanced toward the RV. As he did, a station wagon passed by. Its wheels hissed and then thumped in a pothole concealed within a puddle. But the driver never saw the young man, for he was just another silhouette in a night of shadows.

The stranger stepped up to the parked motor home. It was unlocked, empty, and didn't hold his attention long. Soon, he was walking up the driveway with the confident pace of someone who belonged. Stepping out of the streetlights, he walked in the shadows that ran the length of home number thirteen. Moving away from both the street and the window with the flickering light, he plodded through tall, unkempt grass to the back of the house. Stooping, the young man reached for one handle of the basement's bulkhead doors. Just before making contact, a warm orange spark leapt from his index finger and skipped along the door's metal surface until it disappeared into the wood siding of the home.

He straightened, the rain dripping from his smooth forehead as he withdrew a handkerchief from inside his coat. The stranger wrapped this around his fingers and tried the handle again. The doors were locked.

Glancing around, he could see no lights on in the nearby homes. Under the cover of night, confident there wasn't a watchful eye on him, he approached the steps of the small rear porch. Again using the handkerchief, he turned the knob, and the door opened without a sound. The young man stepped inside.

There was no floor mat in the kitchen, so the rainwater fell from his coat to the old wooden floorboards beneath.

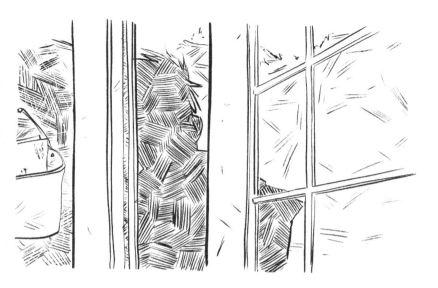

His first step was careful, to determine the noise his weight would make on the worn floor. It was hardly noticeable compared to that of the TV in the next room. The stranger moved when the volume from the current show increased and slowed when it subsided. He advanced this way until he had exited the kitchen and was standing in the entry hall. On his left he saw a couch and the back of a man's head resting on its cushions. When the low nasally drone of snoring could be heard, he turned his attention to the staircase. At the foot of the steps were pairs of shoes belonging to feet smaller than his. The girl's shoes.

The young man sighed, and a glowing maroon spark slid from the corner of his mouth and rolled off his shoulder.

The man on the couch stirred. He adjusted his head and sank deeper into the cushions.

Not waiting for him to settle farther, the stranger moved to the couch. He stood over the sleeper, whose chin had lowered to his chest and whose arms rested limply at his sides. Leaning, the stranger reached with his left hand for the man's throat and moved the fingers of his right hand along the cushions toward the back of his neck. His hands grew warm, and the growing current between his fingers drew them closer together. He noticed this and held still. Raising his hand, he moved it before him and studied the supple skin. Again he looked down at the man, but then turned once more to the steps. Calmly he walked over to the delicate shoes. The young man directed his gaze at the ceiling, where he followed the cracked and mildewed plaster to the front. There, his eyes hesitated on a small area above. This place held his attention for several minutes, until finally he lowered his head, returned to the kitchen, and stepped back out into the night.

20

"Hey Dad, this isn't your foot size is it?" Maggie knelt beside the railing in the front hallway and stared at a faint outline in mud. She was positive that the boot print was not her father's size, but she wanted him to see it.

Please tell me you know whose this is, she thought, as he slowly walked over, *or that I'm just seeing things. That would suck too—but less than a stranger's footprint in our freakin' house! Can you walk a little faster Pops?*

"What foot size?" the man asked. He looked around unenthusiastically for the pair of shoes in question.

"This," Maggie said, "the muddy print on the floor. They're all over the place. The things come in from the back door in the kitchen—which was *unlocked* again."

The man didn't even acknowledge her bringing up the unlocked door. Maggie had asked him several times in the last few years to make sure the doors were secured after she went to bed, but it never worked. The girl locked them herself each night—and checked every window—but if her father went out for a smoke, a chew, or to get something from the garage, he would undoubtedly leave the door he used unlocked.

"Probably from one of the cops," he answered, and started to walk away.

"But they came in the *front* door!" Maggie snapped, the words erupting from her mouth.

The man stopped, but didn't turn to face her. She wasn't sure if he had paused because of what she said and what it implied or because she had raised her voice (something not done in the house, simply because there were hardly ever the emotions to warrant it, positive or negative). Stewart tilted his head, looked down at the kitchen floor in front of him, and then continued walking.

Maggie tensed, angered by his reaction—or his complete lack of one. Her dad was the *definition* of apathy, the embodiment of it. If apathy had enough resolve to hold together some kind of physical form, it would look exactly like Stewart Muntin. She already knew this, but to so casually dismiss the fact that someone had entered their house, to care so little about their safety—his *daughter's* safety—was unforgivable.

This exchange did nothing but strengthen Maggie's belief that getting out was the best thing; for her to assume responsibility for her own life and well-being. She wasn't let down by his inability to protect, or even by his lack of desire to do so (at least not anymore; at that point it was a given). She was upset because he was obstructing her ability protect *herself*. Both his actions and inactions were preventing her from *attempting* to live a safe life.

Unacceptable, she thought.

Maggie's bottom lip quivered. She held it with her teeth and went upstairs to finish packing.

21

There wouldn't be a going-away party for Maggie, and she didn't want one. This wasn't just a hollow reaction, or her being defensive; she genuinely was not a fan of parties. As an introvert, the girl of course loathed attention in most forms, but that wasn't quite it; there was a bigger reason. It was that parties had always felt a little pompous to her. Birthdays, for example: they were the most odd. She could never wrap her head around them. Celebrating a day you did nothing? A day you just popped out into the world? If anything, the *moms* out there should have parties thrown for them when it was their kid's birthday. You have ten kids? Great, Mom's having ten parties this year where she won't have to do anything. She'll get gifts and have a nice day all around, *ten* of them. That made sense to Maggie. But a party for popping out? Just weird.

It may have been this attitude that persuaded karma to smother any possibility of a celebration for her. There were no friends visiting to wish her well and urge her to come back soon, or cards left saying that she'd be missed. Most of this, Maggie would admit, was her own doing. She always prided herself on not the quantity of friends but the quality. True, that's what *all* lonely people said, but she honestly believed that quantity equaled being fake. The act alone of pursuing a large number of friends could only be for the wrong reasons. On the other hand, going the hermit route wasn't exactly her intention, but at least she felt she was being real—totally alone in the world, but real.

It took some elbow grease, but the RV cleaned up pretty well. Maggie had used three vacuum cleaner bags getting the ridiculous amount of baking soda out, but it was worth it. The forest-fire smell had diminished to breathable levels, and her eyes no longer teared up when she was inside.

The girl started the engine. Maggie knew the goodbye to her father would be the epitome of awkwardness, so she liked the idea of having something sort of nudging her along. A running vehicle would do just that. He hadn't come out to see her off, so she went inside and found him in the kitchen.

"I left the number to the new school and local police station on the dining room table," Maggie said.

"Okay thanks."

"I'll uh, probably not get in to Marblehead tonight. I'm

thinking about goin' up the 290 and maybe checking out the Wachusett Reservoir. Stopping there and stuff for the night."

"All right. Got it."

Maggie could think of no other way to end it, so she moved in for a hug. Nothing warm and chummy, it was definitely forced, but also something that seemed necessary.

The man made a halfhearted attempt and raised his hands to her back.

Turning away, the girl said, "Well, chat later I guess. I'll check in now and again for sure." But she wasn't sure, really; it just felt like the right thing to say. Something that would make this moment seem a little more normal in the future, maybe making it a bit easier to forget.

Maggie hopped in the RV, put her foot on the brake, and shifted it into drive. She turned and waved up at the house, unsure of whether her father was looking out any of the dark windows. Putting both hands on the wheel, she eased off the brake and left 13 Nicoli Lane behind.

22

Maggie's vision was fine for almost an hour. Her depth perception and focus never weakened, but her left eye did begin to ache.

So let's take a break now hunh? We don't want to go flying off the road, crash through some trees, catch fire, and burn down to a miserable pile of ash—not a jovial pile of ash, but a miserable one. Though I've never seen a pile with a smile. I'm rhyming. Great. I better pull over before this gets out of hand.

She continued driving and went through Rockville, Connecticut, until she turned off Interstate 84. Though the suburbs were usually a safe place to stop (areas with more eyes often were less likely to attract bad people—at least in theory), Maggie decided to pass them up. The girl figured it was more probable that the cops would be called on *her*, since not many people liked a strange vehicle parked in front of their house.

Within minutes, she found the far quieter Old Post Road in the town of Tolland. Pulling over to the side, she parked on the dirt shoulder in the shade of some trees.

Maggie stood and pet the dashboard.

"Enjoy the shade little lady. We don't need any hot *Soggy Biscuits* around here eh?"

Stretching, she looked around at the table, couch, and windows, then at the view outside, and couldn't help but feel proud. Her hard work had brought all of this, and it was rare that she actually took a step back to soak it in.

Aloud she said, "Just remember to get off the treadmill every now and then. Look around." She shook her head.

I keep my nose down too much. Gotta be wary of the grind. The girl chuckled. *I sound like I'm forty.*

Maggie opened the windows on both sides of the RV to let a cross-breeze through. She had found that keeping them open while driving was not a great idea. Actually, it was pretty stupid, a bit like inviting a hurricane into your house.

Breathing deeply, she took in the piney smell blowing in from the woods to the east.

Peaceful. Another nice moment. But before I forget, let me chuck some cold water on this bliss.

She checked the doors again to make sure they were locked and felt for the canister of pepper spray in her pocket. She sighed with a smirk.

Okay...ah bliss.

The girl pulled a bottle of water from the fridge and took a sip, simply because it was there and she could. Little moments like this—having things on hand that she needed or could use—made her feel a bit more like an adult. Perhaps it was because she felt as if she was taking care of herself, even in the smallest of ways. Whatever the reason, Maggie cherished these occasions because she knew that over time they added up. They built confidence and helped shape who she was.

The girl sat down on the couch. The cool breeze nudged a few silvery locks about her face and must have carried with it some pollen, for she sneezed twice.

"Bless me."

Maggie wiped the corner of her mouth and her mind clouded over a bit. The pine smell and the trees nearby brought her back to that night on Elmore Drive.

The woman in the coma.

She knew she had been admitted in that state, but had never heard of her release.

I hope she was released. There's no way she's still there. It was probably just a shock-induced coma—if there is such a thing.

Using her phone, she looked up Hickins Hospital online and clicked on the phone number link at the bottom of the website. It started to ring.

"Hickins Hospital reception," a woman answered.

"Yeah hi. I'm just calling and checking in on um...the woman that was assaulted and brought in to—"

"I'm sorry, what was your name?" the receptionist asked, her voice cold.

"I'm Maggie. Maggie Muntin."

"Are you *family*?"

Maggie paused, not wanting to lie, but before she could respond, the woman spoke again.

"Will you please hold?"

"Sure," Maggie said, and was met by the standard horrendous hold music before she had even finished saying the word.

A few minutes went by, and the girl found herself walking around and fiddling with objects in the RV. She checked the seal of the refrigerator (a perfect fit all around), tested the table for any wobble (there was less than none), and popped open the top cabinet above the side entry door (there was something inside it).

Her brow creased as she stood on tiptoe to see what had been left in there. This particular cabinet was one of the few she had not yet used to store her things. She figured the item in question was probably an atlas Mr. Peppersnach had forgotten about.

Or a kilo of his toxic tobacco.

But it was neither. It *was* a book, though it had nothing to do with the country's highway system. Maggie took it down and could already smell the aged, sour pages inside.

"*Spirits, Specters, and Savages of New England*, by Wilbur Bickentree," she read, and then whispered, "old."

Opening the cover, the girl turned to the copyright page, being careful of its yellowed interior. "Eighteen seventy-seven! Holy smackers—this is worth some *dough*."

"Hello? Are you a member of the Bradley family?"

The voice startled Maggie, and before thinking about it, she found herself saying, "Yes."

"Okay well, some of you are already here," a woman

continued. This was a different receptionist, not the one Maggie had first spoken to; she could tell by how pleasant she was. "I don't know how many of the Bradleys just walked past here, but they're on their way back now to see her. Is that what you wanted to know Miss?"

"Uh actually I'm out of town and I couldn't make it in. I just wanted to get sort of an update on her condition, and to see how she was doing. I was hoping she'd been released by now."

There was an uncomfortable pause. It made Maggie wonder if she had been put back on hold or if they had been disconnected. Not hearing any mind-numbing easy listening, she opened her mouth to speak, but stopped when she heard paper tearing in the background. There was a muffled, "Thank you," and a loud rustle as the woman moved the phone back to her mouth.

"*Discharged?* Oh honey there's no way. You haven't been in here yet have you? She's still out the poor thing. Mumbling. Her family writes down some of the stuff she says, can't make heads or tails of it. And her eyes haven't gotten better."

"What happened to her eyes?" Maggie asked.

"No color, white as the clouds."

The words struck the girl, and it took a moment for her to gather her thoughts. "And what have the doctors said about that? Did they say what might be happening to her eyes? Is there a connection to the co—"

"I'm sorry dear, you're just gonna have to come in for this

okay? I can't get into things any more on the phone. I'm not supposed to say *anything* honestly, but since you're family..." The woman paused, and Maggie felt a pang of guilt.

"Right," she answered. "Well, thank you very much ma'am for your time. Have a good day."

"You as well."

Maggie switched off her phone, walked to the front of the RV, and angled the rearview mirror up to her face. She stared into her milky white eye. Blinking, the girl leaned closer to the reflection of that opaque thing.

It doesn't hurt now. It's not getting worse—I haven't noticed *it getting worse. Damn it.* She let out a breath and sat down in the passenger's seat. *Maybe you need* both *of them messed up to be in trouble—or more trouble. Let's hope it's that.*

She closed her left eye and rubbed her finger against the lid, knowing the act was naïve, but still hoping that something would just wear off.

But it didn't, it only ached.

23

She wasn't there.

The young man had waited patiently, as still as a boulder, hidden in the brush between two properties on Nicoli Lane. He remained there until the shadows around him lengthened and the moon inched its way into the sky.

The large vehicle hadn't been out front. This got his attention, but he was still confident that the girl was here. Not *his* girl, not the one he had been looking for, but something close.

After climbing a column on the back porch, the stranger walked across its roof and grew concerned. Looking through one of the windows, he could see into the room on the far side of the house, the one he had sensed her in the night before. It was dark, save for a little moonlight that found its way through the front. There was no movement inside.

The stranger leaned his forehead against the glass to get a better view of the spare room before him, and the windowpane cracked. He drew back, raised his arm, and pushed the glass in the rest of the way. It shattered and chimed in the air as it fell, then landed softly on the carpet below. A fragment had sliced open the palm of his right hand, but no blood flowed from the wound.

"Maggie?" a voice called faintly from downstairs.

The young man climbed in and more glass fell from the frame. He walked through the hallway and then into the room at the front of the house, her room. His first impression had been correct: it was empty. No girl, no books, and no shoes; nothing.

The young man's left arm twitched as he circled the area. Looking out the front window, he saw that the street was still clear. When his arm stopped shaking, he began to blink rapidly. Attempting to ignore this, the stranger checked the closet but it, too, was empty. She wasn't coming back. True, the man downstairs had called her name, but without confidence. She wouldn't be returning.

The stranger tried to cough, but there wasn't any sound, although his chest heaved nonetheless. Then, moving of its own accord, his left arm curled tightly to his stomach. He struggled to pull it down as small bursts of yellow-green energy fell from his ears. This current tumbled down his back, only to be absorbed by a pulsing yellow light that emerged from his spine. That light flickered and popped like static until it took the shape of bones and a spinal column—though far too large to be human. It arched from his back, each vertebra twisting against its neighbor until the end swung free from the young man's leg. This radiant tail extended to more than six feet and then rose up, twirling past his shoulder and down his front, where even more of it broke free from his body. Reaching out with both hands, he attempted to rein it in, but as he did so, a blue network of glimmering fibers pushed out from his side. Radial, median, and ulnar nerves squirmed and stretched to form a grotesque semblance of an arm, but it was small, almost like a child's.

The young man was close to lashing out, to striking the wall in frustration or pushing out another window, but he knew it wouldn't help. He would find her. Closing his eyes, he repeated this again and again. He would find her. The stranger stood and moved his hands to where he felt the outpouring energies shift. With nimble fingers, he coaxed the sparkling things to his chest, drew them to his face, and took them in.

When he opened his eyes, red and blue lights flared across the ceiling. But they were coming from outside, not from him. The police had been called. There was a car on the street and two men approaching across the lawn.

He dashed across the hall and ducked low as he dove through the spare room window. The remaining glass shattered as his back struck both meeting rails. He spread his limbs in midair and hit the ground hard, landing on his left side. Rolling over his shoulder, the stranger's right foot went through the old wooden fence at the back of the property.

The exterior light of house number fifteen came on as he pulled his leg free and stood. He moved toward the fence and rotten splinters fell to the glass-strewn lawn. With one quick movement, he vaulted over that barrier and ran along the other side until he reached another. Scaling this fence, he found two teenage boys playing horseshoes beneath a porch light. Both turned to him, but the one closest didn't have time to get away. The stranger lunged forward, grabbed the boy's wrist, and pulled him to the ground.

Without looking back, the other boy raced up the porch steps and disappeared into the house.

Screaming and shouting, the captured youth writhed on the ground, his blond hair falling across his face.

Swiftly, the stranger put his left hand over the boy's eyes, and white-hot energy leapt from the struggling youth's form. Some of these bolts sank into the ground, while a few skipped over the lawn and struck a horseshoe post, causing it to ring.

The young man didn't absorb any of these. Instead, he raised his left hand and placed his right on the boy's sternum. A rose-colored glow moved from his fingers into the heaving chest beneath.

The boy was quiet, and all color drained from his eyes.

Pulling him to his feet, the stranger led him around the side of the house. The boy followed without protest on unsteady legs.

The two slowed as they crossed the street. Once on the other side, the deep shadows and tall bushes offered cover. Stepping in front of the boy, the young man leaned forward and released the smallest of sparks from his mouth. This tiny ember didn't dance or meander, but floated straight into the boy's pale left eye. The youth lowered his head after receiving this small flare—as if now this part of his body were twice the weight—and then tilted it to the side. After a moment, the boy straightened and returned the other's gaze. Hurriedly, the stranger waved his arm to the west and the boy walked off into the night.

Eleven minutes later, the young man in the peacoat found a woman swaying on a sidewalk. He offered her a similar glowing cinder and ushered her in another direction.

24

It had been too late to take in the scenery of the Wachusett Reservoir, so Maggie turned off Interstate 290 and pulled into the parking lot of a SuperSaverMart in Northborough, Massachusetts. The girl checked the location online and found that the store was just a quarter of a mile from a police station. She liked this. With safety in mind, she drove the RV toward the back of the parking lot (near the main road) and parked under a bank of streetlights, which would keep the vehicle well-lit throughout the night. Once settled, Maggie went into the store and checked with the manager to make sure that overnight parking was allowed. He said it was, and that she might in fact have a neighbor, for someone else had called in to check as well. Twenty minutes after returning to *Soggy Biscuits*, a large RV (with the immodest name *Lyonsballs Express* painted on the front) parked beside a greenbelt a few dozen yards away. As she was drawing her drapes closed, the girl saw an older man step from the vehicle to let his little dog out for a bathroom break. She figured the dog's name was Harley because the man shouted the word over and over and over as he tried to get the animal back inside. Maggie figured that either the dog didn't care for its name or it was almost entirely deaf. After a few more minutes, the dog's hearing miraculously returned and the two went inside for the night.

Maggie brushed her teeth, rinsed her mouth, and then picked up *Spirits, Specters, and Savages of New England* off the counter. She dialed Ernest Peppersnach's number.

"It's nonreturnable," the man answered, without missing a beat.

Maggie giggled. "Good, because you can't have it back. I drove it to Northborough. We had a good first day."

"That's nice. Well I guess if I'm gonna get woken up, it oughtta be by good news."

"Oh dang, I woke you up?"

"Might have."

"Ah I'm sorry," Maggie said. "I know it's night, but I didn't realize it was *that* late."

"It's not. Us old farts just go to bed early is all."

"Well I'll let you go. I just wanted to say that I found a book of yours by Wilbur Bickentree in a cabinet."

"Oh yeah, that's a good one. That stuff was a bit of a hobby of mine back in the old days. You keep it though."

"I sold it online," Maggie said, hoping he wasn't too tired for a joke. But there was slight pause, and the girl started to second-guess her humor.

"Then you just got a free RV."

Now it was Maggie's turn to falter. "The book's worth *that* much?" she asked.

"Nope."

"Oh. Well I still have it. It was just a bad joke. I can send it back if you'd like, no problem."

"Nah, like I said, keep it. If you find any money lyin' around or gold bars, gimme a call though. I don't care if I'm sleepin'."

"Will do. Okay, you have a good night sir."

"Young lady?"

"Yeah?"

"Listen, I'm gonna get a bit preachy here for a second, so just humor me if you can."

Slowly she said, "All right."

"You're a sassy little spitfire, and you're sharp. I know you're all set to go runnin' about the world and such—and you should. Youth is made for that. Runnin' around and figuring stuff out, and making mistakes—hopefully not *too* big o' mistakes. But you watch yourself, all right? There's a lot of creeps out there. Most folks are good. But one out of a hundred, or one out of a thousand is a creep."

Her mind immediately went to the young man in the peacoat and the footprints in her house. She pushed the thoughts away, but now felt a little vulnerable.

"Yeah...I know," she said. "Thanks. I have my pepper spray."

"Well that's good, anything with the name pepper in it's gotta be good. But that don't make you invincible right?"

"Nope. You're right. And this is good information, but it's really depressing, and definitely the *last* thing I want to hear right now being alone in an RV."

"And at night to boot. Hey, did you just hear something?"

"Cut it out!" she cried, knowing it was a joke, but pulling

the phone away from her head to listen anyway. When she put it back to her ear, the man was chuckling. "I have to *sleep* at some point tonight," she added. "You're just getting me back for calling so late. Making sure I don't do it again."

He chuckled. "Maybe. But I'm not lyin' though. Everything I've said is true and I want you to take that to heart."

"I will."

"Fine. Now you just think of cartoons and butterflies for a bit before you go to bed and you'll have good dreams and be out in no time."

"I'm not gonna sleep a wink, and the bags under my eyes will have handles."

"Sure, but you could be an eighty-year-old with bladder problems, so you win."

"Ugh, TMI."

"What's that?" the man asked.

"Too much information," she said.

"Oh. I thought it was a disease. I can pee fine by the way. I was just kiddin'."

"You're actually *adding* to my nightmares right now."

The man laughed again. "Then we better hop off the phone. You take care of yourself, Maggie."

"Thanks, I will."

"And let me know how the ol' girl holds up."

"I named her *Soggy Biscuits* by the way."

"Ouch. She didn't deserve that."

"I *like* that name."

"Figures."

"All right. Good night sir."

"Night young lady."

Maggie rechecked the doors, put a paperback by her bed, and lay down for the night. She hoped it had been a joke about not sleeping, but with everything going on in her life, all the moving parts, the ground shifting beneath her feet, she wasn't sure how long it *would* be before she could relax, or at least breathe a little easier. She hoped to be leaving a lot behind. That in itself could lessen some of the weight she felt, but it wasn't yet the case.

Give yourself time *girl. Just calm the heck down. You're doing twice what most kids your age do anyway. And quit taking the little wins for granted. I hate having to keep telling myself that. They're important. Like drops of water in the desert or something, I don't know. Metaphors. Slow it down a bit. Things are just starting out. But how about some good news? Like there won't be any more bad in my life. Ever. I just got it all over with. Bam. Smooth sailing from now on. I'm gonna be rich, sexy, have a great job, um...what else? Have* bling.

She smiled. Maggie knew this was absurd, and that even *thinking* everything was behind her meant she was almost begging to be jinxed. But she had never been very superstitious and, as a result, sometimes liked to tempt fate. Perhaps as punishment for this, she ended up staring at the ceiling for an hour and twenty-five minutes. Eventually though, she settled down and fatigue got the better of her. When it did, and she had one leg free on the blankets above her, Maggie began to snore.

To be continued in…

not gonna die in the dark: episode two.

Episode 2 preview

Maggie woke at seven after the sun's light snuck between the curtains to find her. She had slept well, though the RV had grown cold during the night.

I need a fluffy blanket, she thought. *Mmm, you can* never *have too many of those.* She then pictured herself walking around in public wrapped up in something thick, maybe a solid two inches of fluff, then pictured everyone else around her doing the same.

The girl stood and rubbed the sleep from her eyes.

Everything seems brilliant when you're half-asleep. By the time you're on your feet, you realize you're thinking like a moron. Usually.

Once she was back on the road and across the New

111

Hampshire state line (she smiled at the thought of it being her new home), Maggie decided to fill the gas tank and get some breakfast at a convenience store. Not the most appetizing plan, but she was in travel mode. This meant rolling with things as best she could until touching down in Marblehead, hopefully sane and in one piece.

After filling the tank, Maggie parked off to the side. As she approached the store, a boy of maybe fourteen was leaving and she held the door open for him. He walked past her without eye contact or a thank-you.

Are you kidding *me? Like I'm a doorman. Who the hell does that?*

She turned to kid as he left and said, "Anytime!"

The boy gave her a dirty look over his shoulder and kept walking.

Maggie nodded as she entered the store.

Yeah, I'm *the jerk. Wish I could take my politeness back sometimes. It's like the losers on the road that don't wave when you let them in. I need a flat-tire power. Just point and BOOM! Or a slow leak, no boom, that'd probably be safer. I don't want them to* die *or anything, just have a bad day. That guy was pretty close to a two-flat-tire-pop-attack, though. Definitely more than one. Hate that crap.*

She took a deep breath and made a turn down the candy aisle. Trying not to make eye contact with the chocolate cupcakes, *the tempting little bastards*, Maggie stopped at the open refrigerator at the end and took out a prepackaged sandwich with some fruit. The girl inspected them both for blue spots or hairy mold, found none, and headed for the counter.

"You got it wrong," someone said near the register. "Not what I paid for, and you got it *wrong*." It was a short woman and she was very, very angry. The young cashier working the register looked almost as if he were in pain while he weathered the verbal assault. "So what are you gonna do about this?" she continued. "I can't imagine you like charging people for your own mistakes—or maybe you do. And now *they* have to suffer? *I* have to suffer for your screwup? *And* pay for it? Bullshit!" she shouted.

The young cashier nervously rubbed the side of his head. This last outburst got the attention of an older woman a few aisles down. Her silvery hair and large glasses rose over a bag of potato chips for a peek, and then almost immediately lowered out of sight.

Maggie stood beside an endcap of air fresheners, slightly stunned, and just took in the awkward scene.

"I can't—" the cashier began, his prominent front teeth showing fully now. "You finished the coffee ma'am. I can't give you your money back if you drank it all."

The woman leaned forward on the counter and exhaled in the boy's face. "I got one pump instead of four—it tasted like *no* pumps. You can't be cheap with the pumps bitch! Get your manager out here right now."

Maggie raised an eyebrow and turned down the aisle to hide a smile. *Yes. That woman needs more coffee.* She looked back around the air fresheners. *The guy's doing a public service cutting her off. Like anyone needs her behind the wheel after four pumps. She's having a meltdown after* two.

"What can I help you with?" the manager said, stepping from the back room to the counter. She was a middle-aged woman with dark hair and horn-rimmed glasses.

"He messed up my coffee and he won't give me my money back. I don't want to raise a fuss here, but I got things to do."

"Okay," the manager said, motioning to the cashier. "Well let's refund the woman's money so she can get back to her day."

The young cashier turned to his manager, unable to speak for a moment, and then said, "It's stuck."

"What's stuck? The register?"

114

"Yeah, it won't open."

The short woman's eyes grew wide. "Oh you're *stealing* my money now?!"

His face losing color, the boy said, "But you drank the—"

"Shut up bucky—I'm talkin' to *her*!"

The manager inserted a key at the top of the register and hit the NO SALE button. There was a loud *ding*, but nothing else happened.

"That was the sound of my money getting stolen," the angry woman said, breathing hard.

"Look ma'am…" The manager pulled a small money clip from her pocket and put a five-dollar bill on the counter. "Please accept this for the hassle here today."

The short woman took a deep breath and put the money in her pocket. As she stormed out, the bell above the door chimed.

Maggie leaned the rest of the way out of the aisle and said, "And that was the sound of unhappiness leaving the building."

The silver-haired woman stepped into the main aisle, giggling. She turned to Maggie. "And I think it just got a little brighter in here didn't it?"

The girl smiled. "*I* think so."

The manager accepted cash for the sandwich and made change from her own pocket. She smiled at Maggie throughout the transaction and wished her safe travels.

On her way out, Maggie slowed as a tall man stepped to

the side and held the door open. He had short salt-and-pepper hair, a mustache as big as a TV remote, and a leather motorcycle vest. Realizing he was holding it open for her and not someone else, she thanked him as she passed by.

Looking around with a half smile, the girl thought, *Everything evens out, I guess. Forget the bad and remember the good—or try to, right? Easy to say, hard to do.*

Maggie peeled back the corner of the packaged food, popped an apple slice into her mouth, and noticed a man sitting on a boulder along the side of the road. The large chunk of granite was perhaps ten yards back from the highway, so he was more than likely waiting for a ride there. But that wasn't what held the girl's attention. Her eyes were riveted to what was coming from his head. It was a blue and translucent mass that writhed in the air as if floating on the breeze. The thing stretched out from his ear for more than a foot and in some ways resembled an intestine. Though it seemed to be glowing—radiating a soft white-blue light—none of that luminescence affected anything around. Neither the back of the man's head nor his thick turtleneck sweater (a strange choice in the early morning sun) was affected by this light. Turning, Maggie saw that no one else was looking at him.

Why isn't anyone staring?

There were two people using the pumps out front, but neither one observed the man, or found his glowing, wiggling, tumor interesting.

The girl stopped at a trash can, positioning herself so that gas pump was between her and the man on the boulder.

The glow is like—

Trying to look casual, Maggie completely tore off the over of the food container and dropped it over the can. She lidn't notice the breeze carrying it away through the parking ot.

—the guy with the spiked hair…under the tree. His face lowed, or something lit it up. But that's not him.

Standing on tiptoe, she peered between the gas pump and he large price-per-gallon sign on top.

It's not him. Why isn't anyone—

Maggie looked around again and saw that the man filling his gas tank a few yards away was staring at her. She nodded to him as calmly as she could, took a bite of another apple slice, and threw the other half in the trash. Pretending this was normal and not a total waste of food, she looked back toward he road and closed her right eye. The man and his luminous growth were still there.

Am I the only one that can—

She opened her right eye and closed her left, and the glowing mass was gone.

Oh. Damn it. It's an eye thing.

Only her colorless eye could see the bizarre shape drifting from his body.

A messed-up *eye thing. The one the asshole in the coat made. He glows and this guy glows and now…*

The girl speed-walked back to her RV, unlocked *Soggy Biscuits*, and leapt inside. She spun, relocked it with a panicked precision, and then pressed her face against the tinted side window. No one had followed. From her position, only a few of the large granite boulders were still in view, but the man that had been waiting there was not. She figured he must be seated on one that was now concealed by the gas pumps. This wasn't good news. Maggie would much rather have her eyes on him than not to be sure where he was.

All of this shit was supposed to be left behind, back in Connecticut. I'm starting fresh *damn it. Why is this—it's like—I'm being* followed *now?* She breathed deeply and let it out slowly. *Hopefully not. Maybe not. At least it didn't look at me. I think that's good. Please just be some craziness going on around here, like an overflow of insane stuff that I'm coming across, a bigfoot or UFO thing. I just happen to see them every other freakin' day. Is there any chance of that being normal? I mean…is there just so much of this unreal mind-bending crap out there that I keep bumping into it?*

That's not great, but at least it'd be better. Then it wouldn't be about me.

Maggie closed all the curtains and debated whether she should drive away now or wait until she saw the glowing freak walk off.

She dropped the sandwich on the counter and started the RV.

"So, somehow...starting over has ruined my life even more."

Hoping to leave her troubles behind, Maggie hits the road looking for sanctuary...but Eden is nowhere to be found.

Attempting to start things off on the right foot at her new school, she finds herself stalked by a series of unnatural beings. This not only puts Maggie in jeopardy but also endangers those who are kind enough to welcome her.

not gonna die in the dark: episode two is another installment in a serialized tale of the supernatural.

an illustrated novel

not gonna die in the dark

rated teen

:episode 3

by adam archer

"I'd totally feel bad for anyone with my life...even if they weren't on the run from a rabid freak."

Happy to no longer be alone, Maggie soon realizes that those closest to her are now in danger.

Can she keep her distance from the obsessive fiend at her heels and every minion he spawns? Or will the unrelenting pursuit of these aberrations stamp out the flames of those she holds dear?

not gonna die in the dark: episode three is another installment in a serialized tale of the supernatural.

an illustrated novel

adam archer's

not
gonna
die
in the
dark

rated teen

episode 4

"I can't keep *running*!"

The relentless Robert Hudsloan leaves a trail of ruined lives as he hunts down Maggie and follows her north to the family home of Susan Westling.

Friends and loved ones fight to survive in the fourth installment of this chilling tale. However, things are far from over. There are many stories still to be told in the series that is *not gonna die in the dark.*

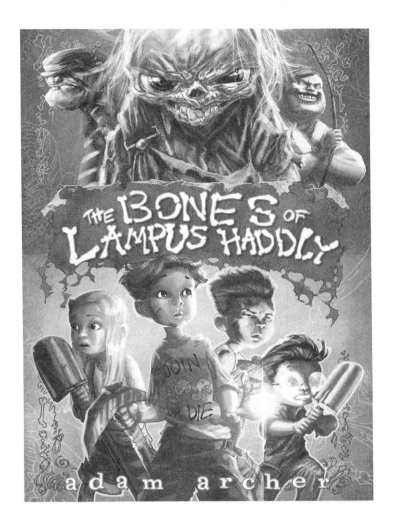

Everyone thought they were going to a normal camp; one filled with sailing, swimming, and wilderness lessons.

But it was all a lie.

For Six kids, Camp Haddly turned out to be nothing short of a living nightmare.

The Williams family thought that leaving the big city for small town New England would be good for them; a relaxing change of pace.

They were wrong.

For on their new property was Lake Nok Barr. At first glance it was beautiful. Its ancient waters were calm and still. That is, until its inhabitants started to claw their way out.

A peaceful galaxy changes forever when five friends open a doorway to an ancient New England graveyard.

Will the vengeful beings they set free destroy the children and everything they know? Will courage, ingenuity, and friendship stand a chance against hatred and supernatural powers?

Probably not—but find out for sure in *The Hoodoo Nic Naks*!

Holly Button was anything but happy when she returned from school to find a gaping hole in her bedroom wall.

It didn't take long, however, for her to realize that this damage was not the work of a mouse. Instead, the origin of this ruined drywall was something far more bizarre.

Join Holly as both friend and foe sail into her life from a distant world.

What would you do if you were camping out with a friend and your body was stolen? Follow that giant, creepy, thief into the most dangerous land around of course!

Join Wilbur and Irene as they journey into the Neverback to battle ghouls, beasts, and at times, even each other.

How would you like it if you woke up one morning
and your breakfast had teeth marks in it?

I certainly wouldn't like it, and neither did Daisy!

Read along as the little lady tracks down the
breakfast bandit and makes a new friend.

32 pages in full color.

by adam archer

Now you might not believe this—and I wouldn't blame you if you didn't—but this book is about an elf that can travel between worlds.

The elf I'm talking about—the little fellow on the cover with the fountain pen—is named Drippy Inkleton. Inkletons are creatures that love to draw but are almost never seen by humans. That's because they can travel between their world (the land of ink) and ours very easily.

When you open this book, you'll find out what happens when Drippy climbs from a puddle and creates a special kind of magic with a lost pen.

118 pages in black and white.

If you'd like magg
adventures to conti
please leave a revie